"Done!" said Arthur. "I finished my science project," he told Pal.
"Just in time for tomorrow."
Pal barked and wagged his tail.
"It's a human heart," said Arthur. "Can't you tell?"

ARTHUR'S
Heart Mix-Up

by Marc Brown

LITTLE, BROWN AND COMPANY

New York · An AOL Time Warner Company

Printed in the United States of America COM-UNI
First Edition 10 9 8 7 6 5 4 3 2 1
ISBN 0-316-73381-4

Pal jumped up for a closer look.
"NOOOOOOO!" cried Arthur.
Before Arthur could stop him, Pal knocked the
whole thing onto the floor.
CRASH!

"What was that noise?" asked D.W. "Ooooh! If that was your science project, you're in big trouble." Arthur couldn't think clearly.
"I need some air," he said.

Binky was shooting baskets at the playground.
"Hey, Arthur," he said. "Want to play a little one-on-one?"
"No, thanks," said Arthur.
Binky laughed. "Afraid you'll get beat?"

"I can't even think about basketball," said
Arthur. "My heart is broken, and I don't know
what to do."
"Oh," said Binky.

At the park, Arthur ran into the Brain.
"Want to help with the launch?" asked the Brain.
"I'm making history here."

"Sorry, I'm not in the mood," said Arthur. "My heart is broken."
"Oh," said the Brain.

Arthur continued on his way.

"Beep!" said Muffy behind him.

"Double beep!" said Francine. "We're going for a ride.
Want to come?"

"I don't think so," said Arthur.

"What's the matter?" asked Muffy.

"My heart is broken," Arthur explained.

"Oh," Francine and Muffy said together.

A little later Arthur almost tripped over Buster.
"Do you have any mysteries for me to solve?" Buster asked.

"The only mystery I want to solve," said Arthur,
"is how to fix a broken heart."
"Oh," said Buster.

Back in his room, Arthur looked at his project. It was in a zillion pieces. How could he ever put everything together again? Downstairs, the doorbell rang.

Binky, the Brain, Muffy, Francine, and Buster were standing outside.
"We all feel bad that your heart is broken," said the Brain.
"Yeah," said Binky. "Who is this girl, anyway?"
"Is it someone we know?" asked Francine.

"Girl?" asked Arthur. "What girl?"
"The one who broke your heart," said Buster.
"Oh!" said Arthur. "Come on in. I'll show you."

"That's it?" said Muffy. "*That's* your broken heart?"
Buster took a closer look. "It is in pretty bad shape," he admitted. "But we can fix it, I think."
"There's no time," said Arthur. "It's due tomorrow."

"We can do it," said the Brain, "if we all work together."
"Yeah!" said Francine. "We'll need a bottle of glue."
"Maybe two bottles," said Binky.
"I'll help with the snacks!" added Buster.

It took a while, but finally they were done.
"Finished," said Francine.
"Good as new," said Buster.
"Actually, it is new," the Brain pointed out.
"Whatever," said Muffy.

"Thanks," said Arthur. "I couldn't have done it alone."
"*Really*?" asked Binky.

Arthur smiled. "Cross my heart," he said.